MW00907376

I Saw an Ant in a Parking Lot

For Emily, my one and only Liebe -J.P.

For my wife, Aymone -M.P.

Library of Congress Cataloging-in-Publication Data

Prince, Joshua.
I saw an ant in a parking lot / by Joshua Prince ; illustrated by Macky Pamintuan.
p. cm.
Summary: Dorothy Mott, a parking lot attendant, must think fast to save an ant
who is looking for goodies right in the path of a minivan.
ISBN-13: 978-1-4027-3823-4
ISBN-10: 1-4027-3823-4
[1. Ants—Fiction. 2. Parking lots—Fiction. 3. Stories in rhyme.] I. Pamintuan, Macky, ill. II. Title.

PZ8.3.P934Iar 2006
[E]—c22
2006005291

1 2 3 4 5 6 7 8 9 10

Published by Sterling Publishing Co., Inc.
387 Park Avenue South, New York, NY 10016
Text © 2007 by Joshua Prince
Illustrations © 2007 by Macky Pamintuan
Designed by Randall Heath
Distributed in Canada by Sterling Publishing
c/o Canadian Manda Group, 165 Dufferin Street,
Toronto, Ontario, Canada M6K 3H6
Distributed in the United Kingdom by GMC Distribution Services,
Castle Place, 166 High Street, Lewes, East Sussex, England BN7 1XU
Distributed in Australia by Capricorn Link (Australia) Pty. Ltd.
P.O. Box 704, Windsor, NSW 2756, Australia

Sterling ISBN-13: 978-1-4027-3823-4
ISBN-10: 1-4027-3823-4

For information about custom editions, special sales, premium and
corporate purchases, please contact Sterling Special Sales
Department at 800-805-5489 or specialsales@sterlingpub.com.

I Saw an Ant in a Parking Lot

By Joshua Prince

Illustrated by Macky Pamintuan

Sterling Publishing Co., Inc.

New York

Well, I saw an ant in a parking lot.
The sun was high,
the pavement hot.
He was walking along, not caring a jot,
a little black ant in a big black plot.

Now an ant's objective in a lot
   is not to park
   but to find a spot
of sticky soda, crumbs, or what
some careless kids or crows forgot.

How do I know? I'm Dorothy Mott—
  the ticket matron
  of the lot.
I gather tickets, punch the clock,
and help lost parkers find their spots.

PARKING
LOT A

And on this morning (August hot),
    in my booth
    (upon the lot),
I sat with doughnut, coffeepot,
tickets ready, parkers sought.

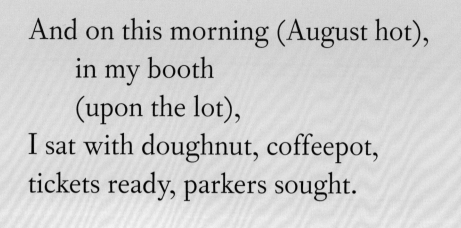

When in came rolling to my lot
    a mom, two kids,
    and tiny tot,
all safety-belted in a squat
red minivan, prepared to shop.

Now minivans are surely not
a mini-peril
when you've got
a mini-ant out on a trot
across a mega parking lot.

But lo and behold, as sure as shot,
   that van turned toward
      the very spot
where, sight unseen (but seen by Dot),
that ant was heading, 'cross the lot.

My stomach turned into a knot.
     Was this to be
     his sorry lot?
To vanish in a tarry spot?
Ant under wheel? A van on top?

The van pressed on—our ant was caught
    'tween rolling steel
    and pavement hot.
Between a mom, her van, her tot,
his trot, her turn, their fate, a spot . . .

O faster ant! O tire not!
  O tire turn
  unless you blot
the living, breathing life out of
a hungry ant in danger caught!

Though desperate was I, and distraught,
I seized upon
a powdered thought:
A doughnut thrown across a lot
could also be . . .
a *warning* shot.

Now you're thinking! Nice one, Dot!
You've hatched a plan,
but dally not.
The wheels are turning (so's the plot).
Give doughnut wings—it's worth a shot!

And so I summoned all I've got
    to hurl a powdered
    jelly-knot
above the lanes at just the spot
across that steaming parking lot.

Skyward . . . vanward . . . antward . . . SPLOT!

That sticky missile
hit the spot
just east of anguish, west of caught,
north of trouble, south of shot.

The ant gave chase! The van did not!
    Braking fast,
    it came to stop
with screeching tires, squeals from tot,
just inches from ant's breakfast spot.

Score: Dorothy 1, disaster naught!
　　An ant alive,
　　　a van in spot!
A doughnut shared and coffee hot.
All is well in Dorothy's lot.